Cat Tails

Pam Scheunemann

Illustrated by Neena Chawla

Consulting Editor, Diane Craig, M.A./Reading Specialist

ABDO
Publishing Company

Published by ABDO Publishing Company, 4940 Viking Drive, Edina, Minnesota 55435.

Printed in the United States.

E Scheunem
Scheunem

Credits
Edited by: Pam Price
Curriculum Coordinator: Nancy Tuminelly
Cover and Interior Design and Production: Mighty Media
Photo Credits: Brand X Pictures, Digital Vision, Eyewire Images, ShutterStock

Library of Congress Cataloging-in-Publication Data

Scheunemann, Pam, 1955-
    Cat tails / Pam Scheunemann ; illustrated by Neena Chawla.
        p. cm. -- (Fact & fiction. Animal tales)
    Summary: Silky and Angel, feline detectives assigned to Pooch Patrol, investigate a rumor that the Bowser Bunch dog pack is planning to take over Purrsville. Includes facts about cats.
    ISBN 1-59679-927-7 (hardcover)
    ISBN 1-59679-928-5 (paperback)
    [1. Detectives--Fiction. 2. Cats--Fiction. 3. Dogs--Fiction. 4. Mystery and detective stories.]
    I. Chawla, Neena, ill. II. Title. III. Series.

    PZ7.S34424Cat 2006
    [E]--dc22

                                                                2005027826

SandCastle Level: Fluent

SandCastle™ books are created by a professional team of educators, reading specialists, and content developers around five essential components—phonemic awareness, phonics, vocabulary, text comprehension, and fluency—to assist young readers as they develop reading skills and strategies and increase their general knowledge. All books are written, reviewed, and levels for guided reading, early reading intervention, and Accelerated Reader® programs for use in shared, guided, and independent reading and writing activities to support a balanced approach to literacy instruction. The SandCastle™ series has four levels that correspond to early literacy development. The levels help teachers and parents select appropriate books for young readers.

| **Emerging Readers** | **Beginning Readers** | **Transitional Readers** | **Fluent Readers** |
| (no flags) | (1 flag) | (2 flags) | (3 flags) |

These levels are meant only as a guide. All levels are subject to change.

FACT & Fiction

This series provides early fluent readers the opportunity to develop reading comprehension strategies and increase fluency. These books are appropriate for guided, shared, and independent reading.

FACT The left-hand pages incorporate realistic photographs to enhance readers' understanding of informational text.

Fiction The right-hand pages engage readers with an entertaining, narrative story that is supported by whimsical illustrations.

The Fact and Fiction pages can be read separately to improve comprehension through questioning, predicting, making inferences, and summarizing. They can also be read side-by-side, in spreads, which encourages students to explore and examine different writing styles.

FACT OR Fiction? This fun quiz helps reinforce students' understanding of what is real and not real.

SPEED READ The text-only version of each section includes word-count rulers for fluency practice and assessment.

GLOSSARY Higher-level vocabulary and concepts are defined in the glossary.

SandCastle™ would like to hear from you.

Tell us your stories about reading this book. What was your favorite page? Was there something hard that you needed help with? Share the ups and downs of learning to read. To get posted on the ABDO Publishing Company Web site, send us an e-mail at:

sandcastle@abdopublishing.com

Cats spend a lot of time grooming. Licking their fur keeps them clean. It also cools them when they are hot.

Silky is a very special cat. He can change the color of his fur to blend in to any surroundings. Being able to alter his appearance is very helpful in his job as the head detective of the Purrsville Pooch Patrol.

Cats hear very well. They rotate their ears to locate the source of a sound.

Today Silky and his able assistant, Angel, are checking out tips that the Bowser Bunch dog pack is planning to take over Purrsville.

When cats lap up liquids, they use the underside of their tongues instead of the top.

Silky and Angel stop at the café for a cup of coffee. There they see a black Lab dog. "Look how many extra cups of coffee he's buying," Silky says, sipping his coffee. "I bet he's a member of the Bowser Bunch. Let's go!"

9

Cats use their tails to communicate. When cats are annoyed, or about to attack, they wave their tails from side to side.

Silky and Angel tail the dog to the swamp. Silky says, "I'm going to blend in and see where he goes."

"I'll stay here, boss, and listen to the police radio," Angel says. Her tail twitches in excitement at the thought of nabbing the gang.

11

The span of a cat's whiskers is about as wide as its body. Cats use their whiskers to see if they can fit through openings.

Silky's fur takes on a leafy pattern. He crawls through a hollow log as he follows the dog. The Bowser Bunch, led by the notorious Big Dog, is gathered in a clearing in the cattails.

13

Cats sleep 16 to 18 hours a day. But they stay alert to danger even when they are asleep.

Silky creeps silently to the edge of the clearing. By now he has taken on the appearance of the cattails. He leans forward to listen.

"We'll have to make our move tomorrow while those lazy cats are catnapping," Big Dog says.

Cats have a sense of smell many times stronger than that of humans.

Silky whispers into the radio. He says to
Angel, "I've sniffed out their plan. I want
you to call headquarters. Ask them to send
over the remote control
Super Stick Cat-a-Pult
right away."

17

Cats love high places. Cats can jump up to six times as high as they are long.

18

The Bowser Bunch dogs can't resist chasing the sticks thrown by the remote control Super Stick Cat-a-Pult. They chase them right out of Purrsville. Silky and Angel high-five each other. "It's another job well done!" they purr with satisfaction.

19

FACT OR FICTION?

Read each statement below. Then decide whether it's from the FACT section or the FICTION section!

1. The span of a cat's whiskers is about as wide as its body.

2. Cats love high places.

3. Cats can change colors.

4. Cats drink coffee.

Cats spend a lot of time grooming. Licking their fur keeps them clean. It also cools them when they are hot.

Cats hear very well. They rotate their ears to locate the source of a sound.

When cats lap up liquids, they use the underside of their tongues instead of the top.

Cats use their tails to communicate. When cats are annoyed, or about to attack, they wave their tails from side to side.

The span of a cat's whiskers is about as wide as its body. Cats use their whiskers to see if they can fit through openings.

Cats sleep 16 to 18 hours a day. But they stay alert to danger even when they are asleep.

Cats have a sense of smell many times stronger than that of humans.

Cats love high places. Cats can jump up to six times as high as they are long.

10
20
21
31
36
46
52
61
71
74
86
97
99
111
118
128
131
142
148

Silky is a very special cat. He can change the color of his fur to blend in to any surroundings. Being able to alter his appearance is very helpful in his job as the head detective of the Purrsville Pooch Patrol.

Today Silky and his able assistant, Angel, are checking out tips that the Bowser Bunch dog pack is planning to take over Purrsville.

Silky and Angel stop at the café for a cup of coffee. There they see a black Lab dog. "Look how many extra cups of coffee he's buying," Silky says, sipping his coffee. "I bet he's a member of the Bowser Bunch. Let's go!"

Silky and Angel tail the dog to the swamp. Silky says, "I'm going to blend in and see where he goes."

"I'll stay here, boss, and listen to the police radio," Angel says. Her tail twitches in excitement at the thought of nabbing the gang.

10
20
29
39
41
49
57
64
75
84
92
101
108
117
127
129
138
145
153

Silky's fur takes on a leafy pattern. He crawls through a hollow log as he follows the dog. The Bowser Bunch, led by the notorious Big Dog, is gathered in a clearing in the cattails.

Silky creeps silently to the edge of the clearing. By now he has taken on the appearance of the cattails. He leans forward to listen.

"We'll have to make our move tomorrow while those lazy cats are catnapping," Big Dog says.

Silky whispers into the radio. He says to Angel, "I've sniffed out their plan. I want you to call headquarters. Ask them to send over the remote control Super Stick Cat-a-Pult right away."

The Bowser Bunch dogs can't resist chasing the sticks thrown by the remote control Super Stick Cat-a-Pult. They chase them right out of Purrsville. Silky and Angel high-five each other. "It's another job well done!" they purr with satisfaction.

GLOSSARY

alert. watchful and aware of what is happening

alter. to change

communicate. to share ideas, information, or feelings

groom. to clean oneself and take care of one's appearance

nab. to arrest or capture

notorious. having a widely known, bad reputation

rotate. to turn on or around a center

tail. 1) a part of an animal's body that sticks out from its rear end 2) to follow and watch someone